This Book Belongs To

. . . .

. . . .

3-MINUTE STORIES

FOR

3-YEAR-OLDS

Cover illustrated by Katie Melrose
Illustrated by Lisa Alderson, Victoria Assanelli,
John Bendall-Brunello, Jacqueline East,
Mar Ferrero, Lorena Alvarez Gómez, Xuan Le, Hannah Peck,
Zoe Persico, Julianna Swaney, and Gail Yerrill
Additional illustrations by Katie Melrose

3-MINUTE STORIES FOR 3-YEAR-OLDS

cottage door press

CONTENTS

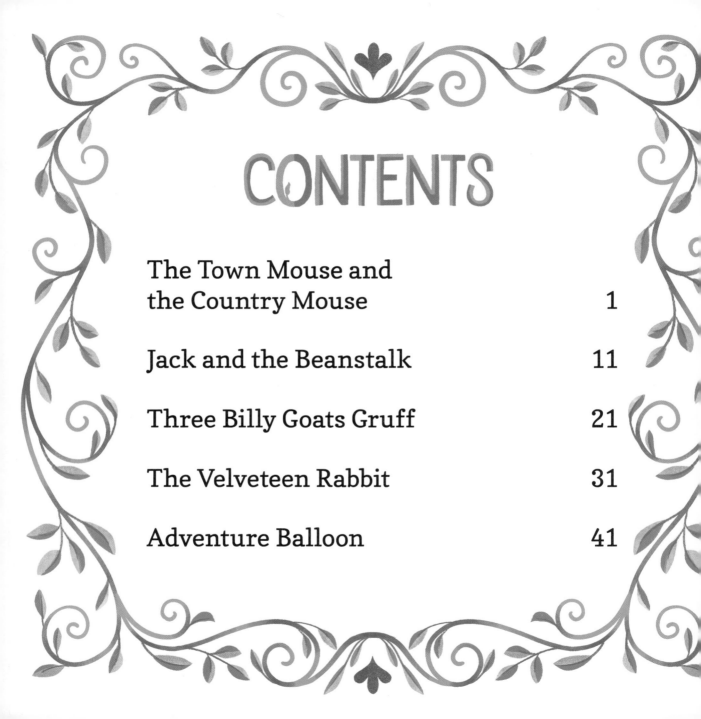

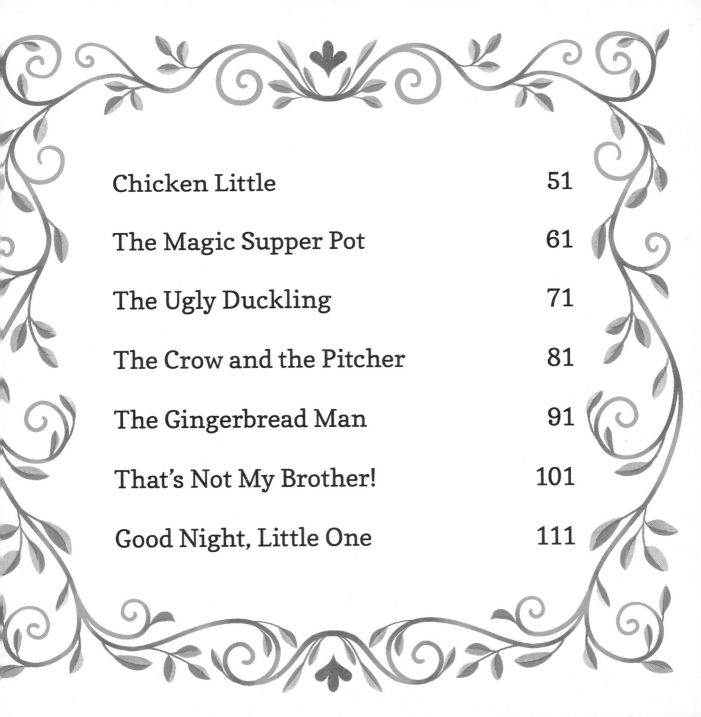

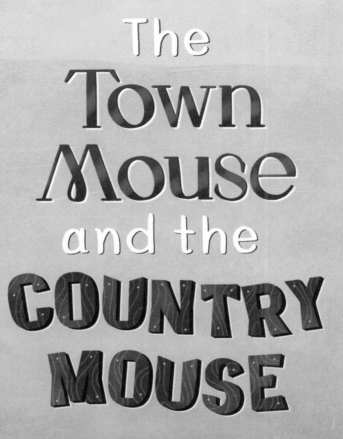

The Town Mouse and the Country Mouse

Illustrated by Victoria Assanelli

1

Once upon a time, there lived two little mice. One lived out in the country and loved the wide, open spaces. The other lived in town and loved the bustling city. Both were happy in their homes.

One day, Town Mouse decided to go visit his friend. He was excited to see what life was like in the country.

"Welcome!" said Country Mouse. "I've made us some lunch."

He set down a plate of mouthwatering food in front of Town Mouse. Though it was delicious, Town Mouse was still hungry when he was finished.

"Ready for a walk?" asked Country Mouse.

"Let's go!" said Town Mouse.

They walked past fields and wildflowers.

Suddenly, Town Mouse heard a noise.

MOO, MOO, MOO!

"What's that?" asked Town Mouse.

"That's just a cow," said Country Mouse.

"They're nothing to be afraid of."

Then, Town Mouse heard another noise.
BAA, BAA, BAA!
"What's that?" he asked.
"Those are just sheep," explained Country Mouse.
"They're nothing to be afraid of."

5

They walked until they came to the edge of a forest. They heard a noise much scarier than the others. HOO, HOO, HOO!

"What's that?" asked Town Mouse.

"An owl!" shrieked Country Mouse. "RUN! Owls eat mice like us!"

The two mice hid inside a hollow log.

"Come visit me in town and you'll see how much better it is than this place," Town Mouse said.

Country Mouse was curious, so he headed to town.

"Welcome!" said Town Mouse. The two mice sat down to lunch. Country Mouse had never seen so many sweets before!

"That was delicious, but now I don't feel well," said Country Mouse.

"A walk will help!" said Town Mouse.

The two mice walked past schools and busy grocery stores. Soon, Country Mouse heard a loud noise. BEEP, BEEP, BEEP!

"What's that?" asked Country Mouse.

"That's just a car," said Town Mouse. "It's nothing to be afraid of."

Then, Country Mouse heard another noise. ZOOM, ZOOM, ZOOM!

"What's that?" he asked.

"That's just a plane," said Town Mouse. "It's nothing to be afraid of."

After walking by storefronts and parking lots, Country Mouse heard another sound. MEOW, MEOW, MEOW!

"What's that?" he asked.

"It's a cat!" shouted Town Mouse. "RUN! Cats eat mice like us!" The two mice hid beneath some stairs.

"I don't think I like the big town," said Country Mouse. "And you don't like the country."

"But we can still be friends and like different things!" said Town Mouse.

So both mice went home. Country Mouse nibbled on cheese. Town Mouse bit into a sweet cherry. "Home sweet home," they said.

Jack AND THE Beanstalk

Illustrated by Zoe Persico

11

Once upon a time, there was a giant who lived in a castle, waaaaaay up in the clouds. Every year at this time, the giant went to visit his mother. He asked a friend to keep an eye on his place.

"Have a nice visit with your mom!"

Also once upon a time, there was a boy named Jack who lived on a poor little farm with his mother. Every year at this time, Jack planted seeds for a little garden. But this year, there were no seeds to be found.

Until one day when Jack looked up and saw ... it was raining beans! Big ones! Would someone big come looking for them? Quickly, Jack planted and watered the beans.

The next morning, Jack checked on his beans.

"Well," said Jack's mother, "I guess you're going to have to climb that beanstalk, and tell someone thank you."

Jack climbed and climbed and climbed and climbed and climbed some more.

When he reached the top of the beanstalk, guess what he saw? Oh sure, the castle. But what else? A beautiful garden full of fruits and vegetables and flowers!

"Hello!" Jack called.

"Howdy-do!" said Dottie.

"Hello!"   "Howdy-do!"

Dottie showed Jack around the place. Jack told Dottie about his farm. And he told her about the big beans.

"Oops!" said Dottie. "I wondered where they went! They must have rolled off a cloud!"

Dottie was sad for Jack and his mother. So she gave him a very special gift to take home.

"The giant would want you to have these," she said.

Jack and his mother planted the seeds and were never hungry again. In fact, no one in the village was ever hungry again.

Thanks to Dottie, Jack, and the giant, there was plenty of food to share forever and ever.

THREE BILLY GOATS GRUFF

Illustrated by Mar Ferrero

Once upon a time, there lived three billy goat brothers. There was a big billy goat, a middle-size billy goat, and a little billy goat.

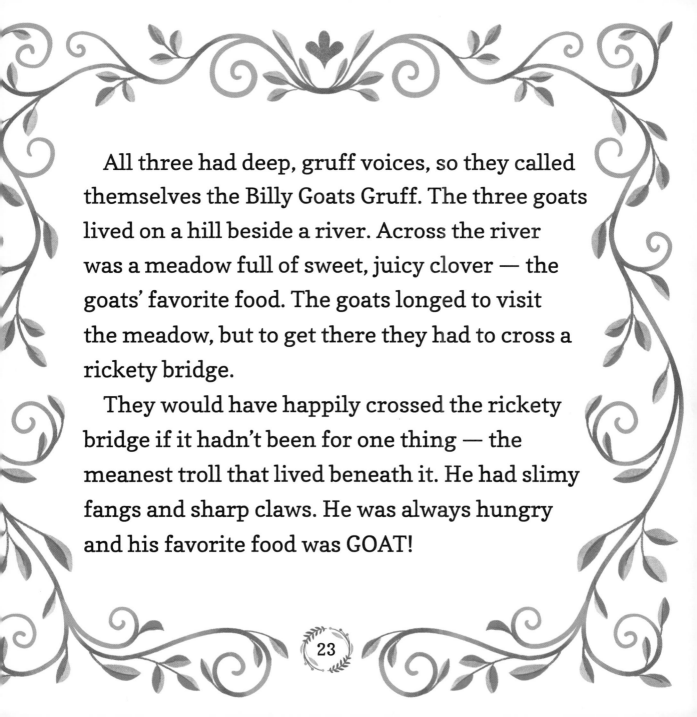

All three had deep, gruff voices, so they called themselves the Billy Goats Gruff. The three goats lived on a hill beside a river. Across the river was a meadow full of sweet, juicy clover — the goats' favorite food. The goats longed to visit the meadow, but to get there they had to cross a rickety bridge.

They would have happily crossed the rickety bridge if it hadn't been for one thing — the meanest troll that lived beneath it. He had slimy fangs and sharp claws. He was always hungry and his favorite food was GOAT!

The Billy Goats Gruff stayed away from the bridge and ate the grass in their field. They ate and ate, until one day there was nothing left but dirt. They decided that they had no other choice but to cross the bridge.

"I'm not scared of that ugly troll," said the little Billy Goat Gruff. So he decided to go first. He hadn't gone far when he heard a terrifying ROOOAR.

"Who's that clip-clopping over my bridge?" roared the troll.

"Only me, the teeny little Billy Goat Gruff," replied the goat bravely. "I'm on my way to eat some clover."

"No, you're not," bellowed the troll. "I'm hungry, and I'm going to gobble you up."

"Please don't do that. I'm small and bony. My brother will be coming this way soon. He is far bigger than me. He'll make a much better meal."

The troll licked his lips hungrily.

"You do look kind of scrawny," he said. " I could wait a little longer for a bigger meal."

So the little Billy Goat Gruff skipped across the bridge and was soon munching on clover on the other side. Soon the middle-size Billy Goat Gruff began crossing the bridge.

"Who's that clip-clopping over my bridge?" snarled the troll.

"Only me, the middle-size Billy Goat Gruff," replied the billy goat. "I'm on my way to eat some clover."

"No, you're not," snarled the troll. "I'm going to gobble you up!"

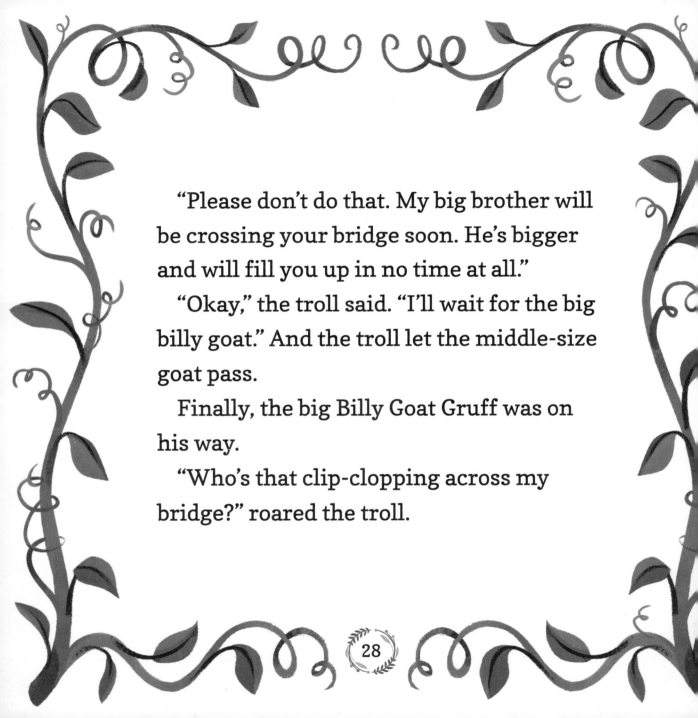

"Please don't do that. My big brother will be crossing your bridge soon. He's bigger and will fill you up in no time at all."

"Okay," the troll said. "I'll wait for the big billy goat." And the troll let the middle-size goat pass.

Finally, the big Billy Goat Gruff was on his way.

"Who's that clip-clopping across my bridge?" roared the troll.

"Just me, the biggest Billy Goat Gruff of all," cried the last billy goat and charged at the troll. SPLASH! The troll landed in the water and disappeared.

Then the big Billy Goat Gruff clip-clopped across the bridge to join his brothers. And as for the silly old troll? Well, he was never seen again!

The Velveteen Rabbit

Illustrated by Jacqueline East

31

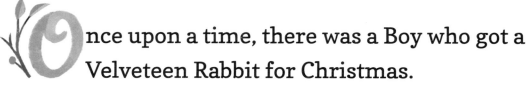

Once upon a time, there was a Boy who got a
Velveteen Rabbit for Christmas.
   The Boy thought the Velveteen Rabbit was
wonderful, but whispered, "I wish you
were real," to the Rabbit
before putting him away
in his toy chest.

"What is real?" the Velveteen Rabbit asked the other toys in the chest.

"It's what you become when a child really loves you," explained a hobbyhorse.

One night Nanny was putting the Boy to bed and gave him the Velveteen Rabbit. From that night on, the Velveteen Rabbit slept with the Boy. And the Rabbit would dream about becoming real.

The Velveteen Rabbit went wherever the Boy went. He had rides in the wheelbarrow and picnics on the grass. One day, the Boy left the Rabbit on the lawn. At bedtime, Nanny came to get the Rabbit because the Boy couldn't sleep without him.

"Imagine all that fuss about a toy," said Nanny.

"He isn't a toy. He's real!" cried the Boy.

When the Rabbit heard these words he was filled with joy! The Boy said he was real!

One afternoon, the Boy left the Rabbit in the woods while he went to pick some flowers. Suddenly, two strange creatures appeared. They looked like the Velveteen Rabbit but they could move by themselves.

"Why don't you come and play with us?" one of them asked.

He didn't want to tell them that he couldn't move. But all the time he was longing to hop like them.

"Wait, he doesn't smell right," the wild rabbit cried. "He isn't real!"

"I am real," said the Velveteen Rabbit. "The Boy said so."

Just then, the Boy ran past and the wild rabbits disappeared.

Weeks and months passed and even though the Boy loved his toy, he grew older and played with the Velveteen Rabbit less and less.

One day, the Velveteen Rabbit was put into a sack and carried to the backyard, ready to be donated. That night, the Velveteen Rabbit was feeling lonely and cold as his head poked out of the sack. He looked around and remembered all the fun he had with the Boy. A real tear trickled down his velvet cheek.

Suddenly, a tiny flower sprouted out of the ground and out flew a tiny fairy.

"Little Rabbit," she said, "I am the Nursery Fairy. I make toys real."

"Wasn't I real before?" asked the Rabbit.

"You were real to the Boy," the Fairy said. "But now you'll be real to everyone."

The Fairy flew with him into the woods where the wild rabbits were playing. The little rabbit didn't know what to do. Then something tickled his face and, before he knew what he was doing, he lifted his leg to scratch his nose. He could move! He was real at last. And off he hopped to play with the other real rabbits.

ADVENTURE BALLOON

Illustrated by Lorena Alvarez Gómez

Eloise raced across the hill.

"You can't catch me!" she giggled. Her little brother Hal was behind her, running as fast as he could. Scruffy, their dog, bounded beside Hal. Suddenly, they saw a big basket sitting at the top of the hill. A huge hot-air balloon was attached to it.

"It's beautiful!" said Eloise. "Let's go for a ride!"

"Hooray! An adventure!" said Hal. "Come on, Scruffy!"

Eloise hopped inside the basket, followed by Scruffy. Hal clambered in after them and then, magically, the balloon began to rise into the sky. They floated up among the fluffy white clouds.

Birds fluttered around them, twittering with curiosity. The green hills and tall trees seemed small and far away. Scruffy wagged his tail.

"Where shall we go?" Eloise called to the birds. Soon, they saw a rainbow-colored tent in a green field.

"The circus!" Hal cried, clapping his hands.

At once, the balloon floated down from the sky, heading toward the field. As it got closer, clowns, jugglers, and dancers came out of the tent.

"Come and join our show!" they called out.

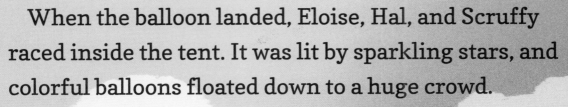

When the balloon landed, Eloise, Hal, and Scruffy raced inside the tent. It was lit by sparkling stars, and colorful balloons floated down to a huge crowd.

"Let the show begin!" cried a clown on stilts. Scruffy did flips and somersaults on the back of a white horse, while Hal tiptoed across the tightrope. Eloise stepped onto the circus swings.

"I want to fly like the birds," she whispered. Then she flew from swing to swing, faster and higher. The crowd went wild.

Later, at the end of the show, the top of the circus tent opened like a lid. Everyone looked up. The hot-air balloon was floating above them.

"It's time to go!" Eloise told Hal and Scruffy. They climbed into the basket and waved to all the people below. Then the balloon rose again. Eloise, Hal, and Scruffy clung to the basket tightly as they soared with the birds, bees, and butterflies.

Suddenly, the wind died down.

"Look!" said Eloise, peering over the edge of the basket. "We're back at the hill again."

Gently, the balloon bumped down to the soft grass, and they all tumbled out. They looked up at the sky.

"That was amazing," said Hal.

"What an adventure!" said Eloise.

Scruffy barked.

She laughed as the balloon seemed to give a little hop of excitement.

"See? The balloon thinks so, too," she said with a smile.

CHICKEN LITTLE

Illustrated by Xuan Le

Chicken Little sat under a big oak tree every day to take a nap. One day, a big acorn fell down and landed right on her head.

"Ouch!" said Chicken Little. "The sky is falling! I must warn the king."

So Chicken Little set off to see the king. On the way she met Cocky Locky.

"Where are you going?" he asked.

"I'm going to see the king," replied Chicken Little. "The sky is falling! He'll know what to do."

"Then I'll come with you," said Cocky Locky.

So Chicken Little and Cocky Locky ran on. On the way, they met Ducky Lucky.

"Where are you going?" asked Ducky Lucky.

"We're going to see the king," said Chicken Little. "The sky is falling! He'll know what to do about it."

"Then I'll come with you," said Ducky Lucky.

So Chicken Little, Cocky Locky, and Ducky Lucky ran on. On the way, they met Goosey Loosey.

"Where are you going?" asked Goosey Loosey.

"We're going to see the king," said Chicken Little. "The sky is falling! He'll know what to do."

"Then I'll come with you," said Goosey Loosey.

So Chicken Little, Cocky Locky, Ducky Lucky, and Goosey Loosey ran on. On the way, they met Foxy Loxy.

"Where are you going?" asked Foxy Loxy.

"We're going to see the king," said Chicken Little. "The sky is falling! He'll know what to do."

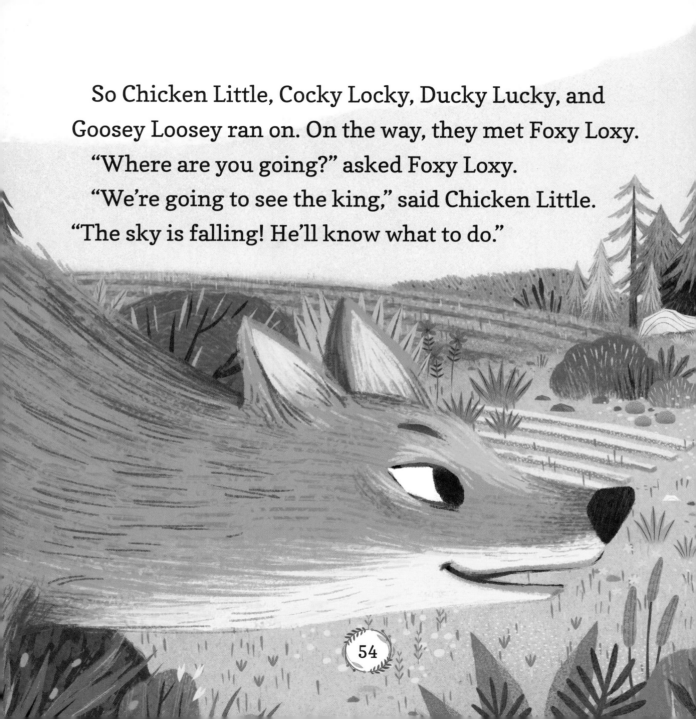

"Oh dear," said Foxy Loxy, with a sneaky grin. He licked his lips. "I do believe you are going the wrong way."

"Goodness!" squawked Chicken Little. "What should we do? We must see the king!"

"I will show you the quickest way to go," said Foxy Loxy, slyly.

So Chicken Little, Cocky Locky, Ducky Lucky, and Goosey Loosey followed Foxy Loxy. Finally they arrived at a dark cave.

"This is a shortcut," said Foxy Loxy. "You will reach the king much more quickly if you come this way."

So Chicken Little, Cocky Locky, Ducky Lucky, and Goosey Loosey followed Foxy Loxy inside.

But it wasn't a shortcut at all! It was Foxy Loxy's den, and he was hungry!

"Now I am going to gobble you all up," he growled.

"Run for your lives!" cried Cocky Locky.

And that's exactly what those silly birds did — as fast as their legs would carry them. And they didn't stop running until they were home.

And as for Chicken Little? She never did tell the king that the sky was falling. Which is just as well, really.

THE MAGIC SUPPER POT

Illustrated by Julianna Swaney

A long time ago, a girl named Abigail lived with her mother in a rickety house in a quiet village. The family was poor, and some days there was no more than a crumb to eat. Although her life was hard, Abigail was good and kind and everyone loved her.

One day, Abigail's mother sent her into the forest to look for blackberries. Abigail searched all day, but didn't find a single berry. She was on her way home when she met a mysterious old woman.

"Take this," said the woman, handing her a copper pot.

"If you're ever hungry say 'Boil, little pot,' and it will feed you well. Then say, 'Stop, little pot,' and it will do as you ask."

Before Abigail could thank her, the woman disappeared in a swirl of leaves. Abigail ran as fast as she could all the way home to her mother.

Abigail told her mother about the mysterious woman in the woods and the magic copper pot.

"Should we try it?" Abigail asked.

"Boil, little pot," she said.

Sure enough, the pot began to rattle and bubble. A delicious smell filled the room and soon there was hot porridge for their supper. Abigail's mother laughed in delight, and they ate until they could eat no more.

"Stop, little pot," commanded Abigail.

The pot became still. The same thing happened every day that week. Abigail told the little pot to boil whenever they were hungry. They grew healthy and strong.

One day, when Abigail was collecting wood, her mother decided to get the evening meal ready. The pot filled with porridge at her command. But she couldn't remember the magic words to stop the pot, and soon it started to spill over!

"Enough, little pot!" she cried, but that didn't work. "Please cease, little pot!" she said. That didn't work either.

Soon the floor was covered in sticky porridge, and Abigail's mother ran out of the house. It wasn't long before the porridge was as high as the windows, then the roof, and finally it came pouring out the chimney and began to fill the street. Abigail's mother watched in despair as one by one, all the houses filled with porridge.

As the sun set, Abigail returned home and saw the village covered in porridge! Abigail knew what to do.

"Stop, little pot!" she called. And it did.

The villagers gazed at the river of porridge in their town. There was only one thing to do — it was time for a feast!

The UGLY Duckling

Illustrated by Xuan Le

Once upon a time, an excited duck was waiting for her eggs to hatch.

"Soon I will have seven beautiful ducklings," she told anyone who would listen.

It wasn't long before she heard a CRACK! And one fluffy yellow duckling popped her little head out of the shell. Soon she had six beautiful little ducklings.

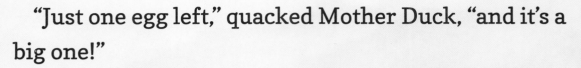

"Just one egg left," quacked Mother Duck, "and it's a big one!"

The big egg began to hatch. Tap, tap, tap! Out came the last duckling.

"Oh my!" said Mother Duck. "Isn't he different!"

The last duckling *did* look strange. He was bigger than the other ducklings and his feathers weren't lovely and yellow — they were gray.

"You're my extra special little duckling. Now come into the water," she said to her tiny hatchlings. "You must learn to swim right away."

One by one, they hopped into the water. But the ugly duckling fell over his big feet and landed with a great big SPLASH! The other ducklings laughed at their clumsy brother.

Back at the nest, the ducklings practiced their quacking.

"Repeat after me," said their mother. "Quack, quack, quackety-quack!"

"Quack, quack, quackety-quack!" repeated the ducklings, all except for one.

"Honk! Honk!" called the ugly duckling.

74

However much he tried, he couldn't quack like his brothers and sisters.

"I'm sure you'll get the hang of it soon enough," soothed Mother Duck.

"I'll never fit in," he thought.

As the days passed, the other ducklings began to tease their ugly brother.

"Just look at his dull feathers," said his sister. "He's so ugly!"

The ugly duckling looked at his reflection. "Why don't I look the same as them?" he wondered. Feeling sad and lonely, he swam down the river and didn't stop until he'd reached a place he'd never seen before.

"I'll be better off staying here by myself," he decided.

Summer turned to autumn, then snow fell heavily that winter and the river froze solid.

"At least I can't see my ugly reflection anymore," he thought to himself.

Then spring arrived and the ice thawed. New visitors arrived on the river. The ugly duckling watched as some magnificent white birds swam toward him.

"You're very beautiful ducks," he told them.

"We're not ducks," laughed the elegant creatures. "We're swans — just like you!"

The ugly duckling didn't know what they meant. He looked at his reflection in the river and saw beautiful white feathers and an elegant long neck.

"Is that really me?" he asked. He had changed so much!

"Of course," they said. "Come swim with us!"

The young swan was overjoyed to have friends at last. As he glided gracefully up the river, he swam past a family of ducks. Mother Duck recognized him right away.

"I always knew he was special," she said, gazing at him proudly.

The beautiful young swan finally felt as though he belonged.

The CROW and the PITCHER

Illustrated by Hannah Peck

It was a scorching summer day in the meadow, and Crow sat in his favorite oak tree. Crow felt as though his black feathers were melting in the unbearable heat. He tried to swallow, but his throat was scratchy and dry.

He flew down to a large rock beside the stream. As he landed, he knocked a pebble into the stream and cool water splashed his feet.

He was just about to dip his beak into the water, when there was a sudden whooshing sound from above.

A hawk was zooming through the air toward him, and he looked hungry. Crow flapped his wings and managed to leap out of the way just in time.

"I'll get you next time!" the hawk called.

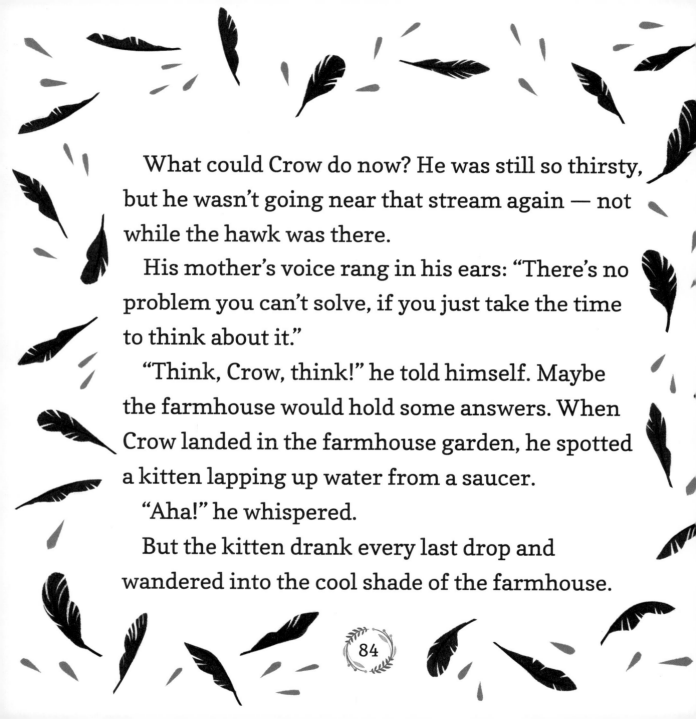

What could Crow do now? He was still so thirsty, but he wasn't going near that stream again — not while the hawk was there.

His mother's voice rang in his ears: "There's no problem you can't solve, if you just take the time to think about it."

"Think, Crow, think!" he told himself. Maybe the farmhouse would hold some answers. When Crow landed in the farmhouse garden, he spotted a kitten lapping up water from a saucer.

"Aha!" he whispered.

But the kitten drank every last drop and wandered into the cool shade of the farmhouse.

Crow glanced around in despair, then he spotted a tall pitcher standing on a table. Crow flew over and peered inside the pitcher. It was tall and narrow. Halfway down he could see the glint of — water! He poked his beak inside the pitcher and stuck out his tongue. But no matter how hard he tried, he couldn't reach the water.

He sank back on his clawed feet and gave a little sob. Just then, there was a crunch of pebbles as the farm dog ran into the yard. Pebbles! That was it! He flew down and picked up a pebble, then dropped it into the pitcher. Clunk! He peered inside. The water had risen. Not by much, but it was a start.

Crow added more pebbles to the pitcher. With each one, the water started to rise until it reached the top.

"Success!" Crow cried as he gulped down a long, glorious drink at last. Crow drank until his feathers had cooled, then he flew home to his favorite branch in the oak tree. The hawk was gone.

As Crow's feet settled into his tree, he remembered his mother's voice again.

"There's no problem you can't solve if you just take the time to think about it."

The
GINGERBREAD
MAN

Illustrated by Gail Yerrill

Once upon a time, a little old man and a little old woman lived in a cottage near the river. One morning, the little old woman decided to bake a gingerbread man as a special treat.

She mixed the ingredients, rolled the dough, and used the cutter to shape it into a little man. She made some icing for his eyes and mouth, then the gingerbread man was ready for the oven.

Soon, the gingerbread man was baked and the little old woman opened the oven. But the gingerbread man jumped up and ran through the open kitchen door.

"Stop!" cried the old woman, running after him. "I want to eat you."

But the gingerbread man didn't want to be eaten.

"Run, run as fast as you can. You can't catch me, I'm the gingerbread man!" he chanted.

The gingerbread man
ran past the little old man.

"Stop!" cried the little old man. "I want to eat you."

"I've run from a little old woman and I can run away
from you," he said. "Run, run as fast as you can. You
can't catch me, I'm the gingerbread man!"

The little old man and the little old woman chased the
gingerbread man into the yard.

As he ran, he passed a pig.

"Stop!" snorted the pig. "I want to eat you."

"I've run away from a little old woman and a little old man, and I can run away from you," he said. "Run, run as fast as you can. You can't catch me, I'm the gingerbread man!"

The pig chased the gingerbread man, followed by the little old man and the little old woman.

The gingerbread man ran past a cow.

"Stop!" mooed the cow. "I want to eat you."

"I've run away from a little old woman, a little old man, and

a pig, and I can run away from you," the gingerbread man cried. "Run, run as fast as you can. You can't catch me, I'm the gingerbread man!"

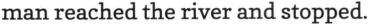

The cow, the pig, and the little old man and the little old woman all chased the gingerbread man.

Next he raced past a horse.

"Stop!" neighed the horse. "I want to eat you."

"I've run away from everyone! And I can run away from you," he said. "Run, run as fast as you can. You can't catch me, I'm the gingerbread man!"

Everyone chased after him. Then the gingerbread man reached the river and stopped.

"I can't swim!"
he cried.

A hungry fox saw
the gingerbread man
and licked his lips.

"Jump onto my
tail and I will take you
across the river," he said.

So the gingerbread man
jumped onto the fox's tail. After swimming
halfway across, the fox said, "You're too heavy for my tail,
jump onto my back." And the gingerbread man did. After
a while, the fox cried, "You're too heavy for my back.
Jump onto my nose."

So the gingerbread man did. But as soon as they reached the riverbank, the fox flipped the gingerbread man up into the air, snapped his mouth, and gobbled him up. And that was the end of the gingerbread man!

That's Not My Brother!

Written by Peter Bently
Illustrated by John Bendall-Brunello

he ducklings were off for their very first swim.

Dora cried, "I want to join in!"

"Come on!" called her brother.
"You're always late!"

And he followed the other
ducks under the gate.

"Where's my brother?" cried Dora.

"Lost your brother?" asked Frog. "I heard a few quacks.
And look! I am sure those are brother-duck tracks!"

So off Dora waddled, with Frog beside her, till they came
to a spot where the path was wider.

"He's here!" Dora cried as she looked up and saw that the
tracks led right up to a big nest of straw.

"That's not my brother!"she cried. "It's Hen!"

"Lost your brother?" smiled Hen, with a chirpy cluck-cluck.

"Those tracks in the straw might just bring you more luck!"

"It's this way!" cried Frog. "Come along, little buddy!"

"Are you sure?" questioned Dora. "It looks kind of muddy."

They heard something squealing behind a big tree, and Frog said, "That sounds like your brother to me!"

"That's not my brother!"cried Dora. "It's Pig!"

"Lost your brother?" said Pig, in his cool muddy hollow.

"Look, there are other fresh tracks you can follow!"

The grass was so tall that they kept falling over as they followed the tracks through a big field of clover.

"I don't think that these tracks are a duckling's, do you?" said Dora, as a very loud voice answered …

"MOO!"

"That's not my brother!" cried Dora. "It's Cow!"

"Lost your brother?" said Cow, as she chewed on her dinner. "Try those little tracks, where the grass is much thinner."

Dora took Frog on a piggyback ride all the way to the barn, where the tracks led inside.

"Found him!" cried Frog. "He just dashed through the door to nibble a few grains of wheat off the floor!"

"That's not my brother!" cried Dora. "It's Mouse!"

"Lost your brother?" squeaked Mouse. "These tracks are ours. But who made those prints over there by the flowers?"

"He's here in the garden, right under our noses!" said Frog as they followed the tracks through the roses. And then the tracks stopped. Frog declared, "Look, his feet! Your brother is hiding behind that pink sheet!"

"That's not my brother!"cried Dora. "It's Goat!"

"Lost your brother?" said Goat, his mouth full of sweater. "If you follow those tracks to the trough you'll do better."

Frog hopped ahead, then he gave a great shout.

"Hey, listen!" he cried. "Who's that splashing about?"

Dora quacked happily, "That must be him! He's in the old water trough, having a swim."

"That's not my brother!"cried Dora. "It's Puppy!"

"Lost your brother?" yapped Puppy. "No need to despair! I think you should look by the pond over there."

When they got to the pond there were no ducks in sight.
"But look at these prints," Dora said. "Puppy's right!
They're definitely duck tracks, and so are these others, which
means," Dora grinned, "that I've found all my brothers!"

Good Night, Little One

Illustrated by Lisa Alderson

oday was a great day for Maya. She did all her favorite things: she read all the books on her shelf, played with her toys, helped her dad bake cookies, and rode her bike with her mom. Best of all, she spent loads of time outside with her friends!

She said goodbye to her friends when Dad called her in for dinner. After she ate, Momma helped her get ready for bed. She took a warm bubbly bath, brushed her teeth with minty toothpaste, and changed into her coziest pajamas. Together they read fairy tales about

 brave princess bears with kind hearts that went on big adventures. Soon enough, Maya started to yawn.

"Good night, little one," Momma said, and she tucked Maya under her patchwork quilt.

And then Maya fell fast asleep.

Except ... she didn't.

Thoughts swirled in her head. She wondered about what Dad would make for breakfast the next day. She thought about riding her bike, feeling the wind in her fur. She loved that feeling. But mostly, she thought about her friends. "What are they doing right now?" she whispered to herself.

Maya hopped on top of the covers and looked out her window. In the light of the moon, she could see the pathway in front of her house. And down the pathway she could see a speck of a house in the distance — her friend Max's house!

She wondered what he was doing. Maybe he was sleeping already. Or maybe he was snuggled up in his cozy blanket, just like her! Did Max's mom call him "little one" and wish him good night, too? Tomorrow Maya would ask him if he would share his toy truck or maybe his soccer ball or maybe...

Suddenly Maya felt a breeze through her open window. The trees outside rustled and she heard an owl in the distance. "Hoooot, hoooooot." She thought about her little friend Flora rowing in her boat under the bright stars. Flora always sleeps while the sun is up, so her day was just beginning. "She's like one of the brave princesses in my storybooks," thought Maya.

Just then she yawned again and felt her eyelids getting heavy. She snuggled on top of her quilt and did what she always did before falling asleep: she thought about what she would dream about. "Tonight, I'll dream about my friends," she said quietly.

And so she did. She dreamed about playing soccer with Max and baking a cake with Dad and riding scooters with Momma and being brave and going on an adventure with Flora in her boat. Her dreams filled her head and her heart, just like all the other little ones in the town around her, dreaming their favorite dreams beneath the light of the moon.